Book One in The JACK REACHER Cases

AuthorDanAmes.com

# SUGAR

## A WADE CARVER THRILLER

## DAN AMES

Copyright © 2018 by Dan Ames

All rights reserved.

Published by Slogan Books, Inc., New York, NY.

# FREE BOOKS AND MORE

## Would you like a FREE copy of my story BULLET RIVER?

### Then sign up for the DAN AMES BOOK CLUB:

### AuthorDanAmes.com

# SUGAR

A Wade Carver Thriller #2

by

Dan Ames

# 1

They came for me in the early morning hours.

A little bit surprising for a bunch of drug dealers. For them, the early morning hours were usually their prime selling and dealing time. Then again, my uninvited guests probably weren't the dealers themselves, but their enforcers. It all depended on the size and scope of their businesses. How well they'd managed to staff up.

Or not.

The reason I was awake, and the motivation for setting my alarm to silent mode was that I had a strong suspicion my snitch, a weasely little guy nicknamed Hammerhead, had flipped.

There had been some warning signs. A bit of weird conversation. Some less-than-normal facial expressions.

Plus, a few things he'd said that were totally out of character for the snide, sniveling, cowardly little addict I'd converted into one of my main street sources in the Delray Beach area.

I would deal with him later.

The other thing that surprised me about my early morning intruders, and probably shouldn't have, was the lack of forethought and planning they were displaying.

They knew me.

Or, at least, had to know *of* me.

If they were who I thought they were, I'd killed two of their coworkers a while back. Granted, they might not have had any actual proof.

Only suspicions.

But still.

They knew I was home. Even though I turned the alarm off, my hidden security cameras were still active and I'd seen them up by the garage, on the pool deck and now, in the back of the house outside my kitchen window.

There were three of them.

At first, I thought they would employ some cheap ploy to lure me out.

Maybe set off my car alarm.

Knock on the window.

Call my cell phone and pretend to be a neighbor saying my house was on fire.

So far, they hadn't attempted any of those tactics, which showed at least a very small amount of sophistication.

I figured they might also think a call from somebody close to me would lure me out, but then they probably realized no such person existed.

My sister, who'd been missing for years and who I had never stopped looking for, was one option.

But a phone call from her, if she was still alive, so early in the morning would be too obvious even for these ass clowns.

Ultimately, they resorted to brute force.

Which I kinda figured they would.

They opted for the kitchen window and showed at least a little foresight by bringing a glass cutter with a suction cup so they could cut a nice big whole in the glass while making very little noise. Just a long, slow screeching sound that didn't carry very far.

The trouble for them was, I had put a thin film of reflective material over those windows.

For a variety of reasons.

The film helped block direct sunlight which meant the house stayed cooler and lowered my air conditioning bill. I was also fairly big on privacy, for obvious reasons.

What it meant was, when you were outside, all you saw was a mirrored reflection. No glimpses of what might be on the other side of the window.

So it was a calculated risk on their part. Breaking through a window even though you can't see on the other side is taking a pretty big gamble.

A fairly big miscalculation because that meant they had no way to see me standing just left of the window with my twelve-gauge Mossberg Defender shotgun, loaded with double-ought buckshot.

Even worse, earlier I'd racked the slide and one of those shells, the kind that can create horrific damage to the human body, now stood ready to blow the first bastard's head right off.

## 2

O NE WEEK EARLIER

"THANK YOU SO MUCH," she said.

Her eyebrow was raised and the corner of her mouth was curved into a smirk. Her thank-you had been as far from sincere as you could get.

"You fucked up six months of work for me," she continued.

She looked totally different to me than when I'd last seen her. Her skin, the color of dark chocolate with a cacao percentage well over 85%, was smooth and flawless.

Her dark eyes were wide and expressive, even when she was conveying sarcasm, which I judged to be her mode of expression most of the time.

She had close-cropped hair and was wearing short shorts with a dry-fit T-shirt that hugged every inch of her body that was all muscle and sinew. Her feet were encased in chartreuse Nike cross trainers.

"Communication is the key," I said. "How was I supposed to have known you were working on a case, too?"

Her name was Dominique.

If she had a last name she had yet to share it with me. I had first met her when she was with a low-level drug dealer named the Candyman. I got him arrested and put away for a good number of years on my last case, mainly because he was a piece of crap who had been trying to extort his daughter's trust fund.

I'd nearly put Dominique out of commission, but had instead just let her go. Now, it turned out she wasn't the Candyman's girlfriend, but a lawyer.

She'd been trying to recover some stolen jewelry and I'd waltzed in and blown her case apart.

Still, I wasn't going to let her know I was taking any kind of blame. Southeast Florida is a wild, weird place. You have to move fast, or the crazy can catch up to you.

"Communication?" she said. "You came in like a bull chasing a big red flag or in this case, a pair of tight little orange shorts," she said, referencing the Candyman's predilection for wearing these obnoxious little orange shorts that had made him look like a Hooters waitress. My guess was that he had a lot of male friends in prison right about now. The Candyman was now a pass-around treat.

"I was doing a job," I said. "Not a lot of time for niceties."

Now it was my turn to take the initiative.

"So what can I do for you, Dominique?"

"I want to hire you."

Dominique leaned back in her chair, crossed those shapely legs of hers. They were muscular and I watched with fascination as her thighs snapped to attention, a move I instantly replicated.

If this woman had any body fat, I didn't know where she was hiding it. I wouldn't mind doing a thorough search. Happy to volunteer, ma'am.

"Hire me to do what?"

"I need you to find a boat," she said.

"Don't you want to find a repossession specialist? Those guys know all the ins and outs of repoing a stolen boat."

"It's a little more complicated than that," she said. "There's the boat, and then there's what's *inside* the boat."

She smiled a little bit and her teeth were perfectly white. She had full, gorgeous lips and I found myself once again considering a full-body analysis to determine her body fat percentage. Hopefully performed back at my place.

"Why don't you tell me the whole story and then we'll talk about my fee? That is, if I choose to accept it."

She folded her hands across her midsection and stretched her legs out in front of her. I was pretty sure she was doing it on purpose to distract me. It was working.

"Do you want some water, coffee, anything?" I asked.

She shook her head.

"So here's the deal," she said. "My client is a well-known entrepreneur. He's made a lot of money and lost a lot of money but he's still way ahead on the profit side. He runs his businesses a bit chaotically. I'm just one of his lawyers. He's got multiple teams on multiple projects."

"And what is your specialty within the organization?" I had a feeling I knew the answer. She didn't look like your typical corporate boardroom attorney. The fact that she had gone undercover posing as the Candyman's girlfriend gave me a clear indication of the kind of cases she would be assigned.

"Let's just say that he prefers to work with me on high risk, high reward cases."

"I see."

"In addition to the various businesses, startups, and industries he's involved in, my client tends to diversify his assets quite a bit."

She was taking her time with this in choosing her words carefully, although that cautious discourse seemed to be her default mode.

"In addition to houses, cars, commercial real estate, traditional stock investments, and purchasing other companies, he also collects artwork." She paused for effect. "And by artwork I don't just mean paintings and sculpture. He also collects jewelry, antique items and other things."

She left it open-ended for a reason.

"So he's got a boat full of this shit somewhere? Like a lost treasure ship full of stolen pirate loot? Wow, this is perfect for a Florida PI," I said.

There was no small amount of enjoyment taken on the blunt quality of my dialogue compared to hers. I smiled letting her know I enjoyed the dichotomy and I think she sort of did too.

"Yes. And I know your next question is going to be why hasn't this matter been brought to the attention of the police?"

"I was wondering about that."

"Again, it's a bit more complicated in that one of his business associates re-appropriated the boat after its sale, claiming that my client's finances fell through."

"Did they?"

"The money was indeed paid."

"So this guy took the boat back and it's full of all these

goodies? What's he going to do? Sell them online? Hold an auction?"

Another dazzling smile from Dominique. This was a woman who enjoyed her work and I think I was going to enjoy working with her.

"Not quite that easy."

"No, I didn't think it would be."

"The boat is specially equipped with some custom designs and most of the items aren't on full display."

*Now this is really getting interesting*, I thought.

"Are we talking hidden compartments on a boat?"

"To a certain degree," she said.

I let all this information percolate in my mind.

"So whoever has the boat, may not actually know what's inside."

"Precisely."

"What was the last known location of the boat?"

"A marina in Boynton Beach," she said. "But, obviously, it's gone now. And no one seems to have any idea of where it went."

I tried to hide it but that would work out very well for me because the drug dealer I had just permanently put out of commission had told me, on his death bed, that my sister was in Boynton Beach. And that she was now called Sugar.

"Give me a description of the boat."

She laid out the make, model, size, color and various specifications of the vessel.

In turn, I gave her my fee rate and she agreed to it immediately. There was one last piece of information I needed.

"What's the name of the boat?"

A smile appeared and she said the name with a delicious sense of irony.

"Brown Sugar."

## 3

Now I was looking for two kinds of sugar.

'Sugar,' my sister.

And 'Brown Sugar,' a stolen boat full of probably illegal items.

And both of them were supposedly somewhere around Boynton Beach, Ocean Ridge, West Palm Beach, or least likely of all, Palm Beach itself.

After Dominique left with the signed contract and a receipt for her initial payment, along with an agreement to meet within one week for a status update (I was hoping for a little bit more than just a business meeting) I immediately went to work on the computer.

For obvious reasons Florida has one of the highest boat owner percentages in the country.

Everyone's got a boat.

And if you don't have your own boat you certainly know somebody who does. Which is really the best way to go, because your friends invite you out on their boat, you enjoy it and then they're stuck with the payments, insurance, and maintenance costs while you're back at your pool relaxing after a day on the water.

The first place I went was a backdoor entrance into the Florida Department of Motor Vehicles. The access had been set up for me by a friend of mine and former client. I went into the boat registration and typed in the boat details Dominique had given me. Apparently it was a Sea Ray.

Naturally, the boats were listed by name. It was organized by owner registration numbers, names and addresses.

Dominique had provided most of that information for me. But there were still a few missing links.

Of course, the bigger the boat, the wealthier the owner. And the wealthier people are, the more often they make one of their businesses the owner of the boat. It's more beneficial from a tax standpoint.

In this case it was called Bosso, Inc.

The computer came back with nothing.

That made things much more difficult. It could be the boat wasn't registered in Florida. Maybe it was a European boat registered in a European or foreign country. Or, even worse, perhaps forged documents for the registration had lapsed.

This happens often, especially if the boat's owners aren't going to use the vessel and they simply put it in storage somewhere.

People also do that if they never actually take the boat away from the dock. Some of these big luxury yachts are nothing more than a pied-a-terre, a secret apartment for extramarital liaisons.

If a wealthy guy wants to have affairs with his secretary and can't go back to his mansion or his luxury apartment because his wife might be there, he picks up his lady friend and sneaks out to the marina where he can bang the daylights out of her and not worry about interruptions.

Dominique did not give me a photo of the boat, so I definitely had my work cut out for me.

The job of finding my sister was ground I had already well traversed. All the usual searching had turned up nothing the last couple of years. I was down to looking for her on the street.

Since it was close to sunset I closed down the computer, went into my little office kitchen and grabbed a beer. The office consisted of a top floor of a funky, cool building that had elements of chic Florida from the 1950s.

The sliding glass doors opened up onto a balcony that overlooked Delray Beach.

I sat down, took a nice long drink of beer and thought about the next steps.

As usual, I couldn't help but go back and think about how I wound up here.

And what had happened with my sister.

4

W hat happened to Jenny was my fault.

As is so often the case, at the time I thought I was doing the right thing.

My father, a Detroit cop, had been ambushed by apparent drug dealers. Gunned down along with his partner in their squad car.

Even though I was still young, I was already a fighter and it seemed like from the day I had been born God had gifted me with a never-ending supply of people more than happy to test me.

It seemed every time I turned around someone was coming at me, trying to take me down. It was fear that drove them. I was already bigger and stronger than anyone my age.

So after my father was murdered, some of his cop buddies had unofficially taken me in as his replacement and I had one mission: to find the men who killed my father and make them pay. They were a rough group of men who sometimes bent the law as they saw fit. It was a philosophy I grew to embrace.

It took almost six months to track my father's killers down. Two piece-of-shit brothers who sold their drugs out of the Hyde Park neighborhood. Up-and-comers who thought killing cops would earn them some street cred. It probably did. But it also brought a whole lot more.

Eventually, we got them locked up in the basement of an abandoned building in Detroit.

We beat them and tortured them in rotating shifts for multiple days. And then for the coup de grace, my friends allowed me to blow both of their heads off with a shotgun.

However, it had been my incredibly stupid idea to bring my big sister Jenny there to witness the final payback. Sort of like family bonding over murder. It made sense to a young man like me, who'd grown accustomed to violence and even welcomed it.

She had watched in stunned silence as I executed both of my father's killers right before her eyes. In my mind, being all youth and testosterone, I was giving her a gift.

Unfortunately, what I actually gave her was a supremely dramatic event from which I don't think she ever recovered.

So, when she disappeared not long after, I assumed it was because she realized her brother was a monster.

I was at least smart enough at the time to not immediately chase after her. It was a case of she went her way, and I went mine.

But before long, I started to realize I was responsible for her. As if she hadn't already experienced enough trauma, I had gone and added to it. Mainly out of selfishness. I wanted her to know that I had taken care of her by eliminating our father's killers from the face of the Earth. In some way, I wanted her to be proud of me. Maybe to even have her look at me as some kind of hero.

It had the opposite effect.

So even though I was the younger brother, it felt like I had made her my responsibility. Because of my stupidity.

Eventually, the quest to locate my sister had begun.

And it had never stopped. This was the closest I'd ever come. I had managed to find out that she was probably in Southeast Florida and now I had a possible location and a possible name.

*Sugar.*

I had a feeling that if I didn't take advantage of this golden opportunity, I would have to face the cold, hard truth.

There might not be another.

S ince I was a subcontractor, I wasn't allowed to directly contact the owner of the boat in question.

My boss on this job was Dominique.

She had made that very clear.

Everything I did, all of my movements and reports, would go directly to her. In my mind, I was hoping to personally delivery my reports. Along with a pair of dry martinis and a dinner invitation.

However, that didn't mean I couldn't do my research on the owner of the boat. His name was Joaquin Villabaso.

It was easy to find loads of information on him in the local Southeast Florida newspapers, magazines and social media entries. He was wealthy, flamboyant and somewhat controversial.

It appeared he had made his money in a variety of ways including family inheritance, investments, real estate trans-actions, fashion brands, restaurants, and, of course, a winery. In those circles, if you don't own a winery, you didn't belong.

There were even a few pictures of him on the boat, although the name Brown Sugar was never mentioned.

I studied the photos carefully. One of the images tugged at a portion of my memory. It was the boat, flying its flag proudly, with the edge of a sign in the background and the words "Pro."

Maybe I could figure it out later, so I downloaded the images and printed them off. My next step would be to identify some people in the photos starting with Joaquin. He was slightly shorter than average and my guess at his age was maybe fifty-seven or so. He had thinning hair, swept back, and he was somewhat handsome in a Mediterranean/Latin kind of way.

He had a prominent nose, brown eyes, an angular face and was a touch stocky. Nevertheless, he wore very formfitting suits and bright pastels. Most of the time he was seen with a martini glass in his hand. If he didn't have a martini glass, he almost always had a cigar.

It appeared as well that he very much preferred his companions to be scantily clad. Both male and female. I saw no reports of a wife. And in his photos there was always a mixture of both men and women. Perhaps Mr. Villabaso's sexuality was as flexible as some of his comely companions.

The reports indicated he had a Palm Beach mansion. And a penthouse apartment in South Beach.

Dominique had said the boat was in Boynton Beach, which is a far cry both socioeconomically and culturally from Palm Beach or South Beach.

The only time anyone from Palm Beach or South Beach would be in Boynton, would be if they were buying drugs or were lost.

Nevertheless, Boynton Beach is where I was going to start, because that's where Dominique had steered me.

Additionally, it was where a dead drug dealer told me my sister was, just before I permanently closed him down.

The sun was just starting to set over Delray Beach proper, and I could feel the breeze start to turn. My beer was gone and I decided it was time to do some nosing around. Which meant it was time to visit my number one street source for information on drugs and drug dealers in Southeast Florida.

His name was Hammerhead.

Little did I know that his actions were about to put a bounty on my head.

And make me the target of some of the world's most vicious contract killers.

"**D**ickie, get out here!"

*Dickie?*

Hammerhead came out of his room. Yes, can you believe that? A grown man in his thirties, living in his own little room with his 80-year-old mother. Drugs and a low IQ will do that for you.

"Mom, please refer to me as either Richard or Hammerhead when Wade is here," he whined. "You know I hate the nickname Dickie."

Hammerhead was a little guy, with tiny legs and an average torso. He had thinning hair, a deeply lined, tan face and looked twenty years older than his actual age.

"Why don't you kiss my ass, Dickie?" she said. She tightened up her pink bathrobe and walked down the hall.

"Stop it, Mom!" he yelled after her.

"I'm going to go take a crap that's bigger than you, *Dickie*," she called back cheerfully.

Hammerhead rolled his eyes and held his hands wide, looking at me for moral support as if saying *can you believe what I have to deal with?*

"Don't look at me," I said. "She's got every right to call you Dickie, or even worse."

He ignored my editorial.

"You want something to drink?" he asked. He went to the fridge, grabbed a bottle of beer and sank into a bright orange recliner.

I watched him take a drink of the beer and asked, "Is there ever a time when you're not dumping some form of chemicals into your body? You're like a hazardous waste site in dirty blue jeans."

"I don't need a lecture, Wade," he complained, sneaking a peek at his jeans, which in fact, really were dirty. He'd probably slept in them.

I sat down across from him on a brown leather couch that was wrapped in plastic, making me feel like a tuna sandwich somebody had packed for lunch.

"Did you ever bump into those two guys again?" Hammerhead asked me. "You know. Those two you kicked out of here."

He was referring to a pair of white-trash thugs who were shaking him down for money. They'd put their hands on Hammerhead's Mom, which I couldn't accept. Eventually, they'd come back for more and I'd left their bodies somewhere in West Palm Beach.

"Nope," I lied. "Why?"

"Well, word on the street is they were coming to see you and then they disappeared. Someone found their bodies up in West Palm. People are upset with you."

"What else is new?"

"They've put some money out there," Hammerhead said, a bit nervously. "These people. They're not exactly nobodies, Wade. They're...connected."

"Really" I said. "I feel all special now."

Hammerhead let it go and so did I.

"Why are you here?" he eyed me suspiciously.

"Why are any of us here," I replied, with a Buddhist expression on my face. "Figuratively, that is. Literally, I'm here because I want to know who controls Boynton Beach."

He leaned his head back. "Ever heard of mood rings? The jewelry that constantly changes colors when the light changes?"

I felt like punching him in the face.

But he kept going.

"That's what those drug territories are like along the beach, Wade."

He spoke to me like he was imparting some kind of advanced knowledge.

"One week some scumbag is selling shit. And then he gets popped and the next guy takes over. That dude dies of an overdose from sampling too much of his own goods and then the next one is in. What do they call that, revolving chairs?"

"Musical chairs, Dickie," I said.

"Oh," he took a drink of his beer and seemed satisfied with his answer.

"Look, you're talking about the street-level dealers," I said. "A dime a dozen. And I know that when you're up there buying your crap, you just get your stuff and leave. Come home to your mom's Crock-Pot meal," I added, throwing in a little editorial advice.

"Meatloaf," he said. "She makes a killer meatloaf."

"But there has to be a higher-level dealer who's in charge of that territory," I said. "We all know Miami is controlled by the South American cartel. The rumor I hear is that the Boca Beach stretch is run by the Jewish syndicate. Delray Beach is anybody's guess."

It looked like Hammerhead was falling asleep.

"Boynton Beach is the next level up for these transient dealers," I said. "When a new one moves in, they have to get the okay from somebody, or they get a talking to."

Dickey shook his head, looking like a little sparrow struggling with a squirming nightcrawler in its beak.

"I can only guess," he said.

"Go ahead, I'm not getting any younger but you're getting drunker."

He sighed. "The only name I've heard more than a few times around Boynton Beach is some cripple in a wheelchair."

"A cripple? Jesus, Hammerhead, I know you're a drug addict but could you be any more politically incorrect and insensitive? No one uses that word anymore."

"What the hell am I supposed to say?"

"Handicapped. Or special needs. Or better yet, just say a guy in a wheelchair."

From the back room I heard Hammerhead's Mom yell out, "My son is special needs!" And then I heard her cackling with laughter.

Hammerhead drank his beer and his face turned a little red. It was nice to see him actually have a little spunk, a little pride. I thought he'd washed it all away with his nonstop parade of controlled substances.

"Okay, so there's a guy in a wheelchair who controls or is at least somehow involved in the middle tier of the drug operation up there. Maybe a middle manager," I said.

Hammerhead nodded. "Supposedly."

"This guy got a name?" I asked.

A little smirk formed on Hammerhead's face.

"They call him Wheels."

## 7

The show was about to start.

The Boynton Town Center Mall was home to a Payless shoe store, Dunkin' Donuts, a dentist, dry cleaner, Cricket Wireless, a vaporium, hair salon and yogurt place.

Tucked around the corner was a lone storage unit.

The inside looked nothing like the outside.

To call it a storage unit would be a complete falsehood.

The space had been designed to resemble a luxury garage for exotic sports vehicles. There was an impressive array of equipment. The lighting was dramatic, the floor was a perfectly smooth, painted concrete with color flakes added for effect.

There were large photographs on the wall of vintage race cars. At various points in the expansive room were other vintage signs dealing with highways, cars, and road travel.

The most interesting visual, however, were the men tied down in the middle of the floor.

Their arms and legs were secured by chain to eyebolts

screwed into the floor. Their heads were turned sideways and duct taped to the floor.

The air was filled with music from the garage's excellent sound system.

Currently the track playing at full volume was *Ride of the Valkyries*.

On the other side of the room was a supremely overweight man in a wheelchair. Neither the man nor the wheelchair was ordinary. He had a massive head crowned with a stunningly horrible toupee. He was outfitted with a NASCAR-styled racing suit that looked like a Halloween costume.

His wheelchair was much bigger than most. It was motorized and had a custom paint job with flames. The wheels were oversized, and thick.

A joystick was controlled by one of the big man's flabby hands.

A group of about eight men armed with handguns stood along the makeshift drag strip, a series of white dashes in a row made to resemble a road.

The man in the wheelchair gazed down the length of the path, until his eye settled on the men ahead, laid head-to-head, their exposed necks in the direct line of his tires.

The fat man inched the motorized wheelchair forward. The light fell on the rear tires, which were offset wider than their counterparts at the front of the vehicle, dancing along the special additions that had been installed on the wheelchair's rear tires.

They were metal blades, sharpened, like snow chains people put on their cars during winter.

As the wheelchair now inched forward, the sound of the metal blades going *click click click* on the cement floor intruded on the music overhead.

Midway along the drag strip was a reclaimed vintage racing light and the lights were all now showing red.

As the music built up to a crescendo the lights switched to green, triggered by a remote control switch in the hand of one of the men with guns.

The fat man thrust the throttle of the wheelchair forward and it rocketed ahead with astonishing speed. The sound of the jagged chains on the rear wheels cutting into the cement floor added a percussive track to the music.

The fat man stared down the path with a laser-like focus. Aiming his wheelchair on a precise path and as he approached the two men, he made a slight adjustment.

He leaned forward more until the vehicle hit top speed.

The eyes of the men on the floor bulged with terror as the wheels tore across their exposed throats. Blood sprayed, sputtered and gushed like a car running over a fat possum.

Roadkill, indeed.

The men's bodies bucked and heaved. Their blood rapidly spread across the floor. The fat man's wheels had left bloody tire tracks leading away from them.

He glanced down at them with satisfaction.

But not for long.

He swung the vehicle around, jammed the throttle forward and accelerated into the men on the floor once again, this time at a slightly different angle.

The blades on the wheels shredded whatever was left of the men's throats, and nearly decapitated one of them.

They had stopped writhing.

The blood pool joined together in one stream and ran toward a custom-designed drain in the floor. At the end of the new, matching set of bloody tire tracks, the fat man turned and slowly drove back to the center of the room.

He stopped just short of the dead men.

The men with guns slowly applauded as the leader among them walked up and put a hand on the fat man's shoulders.

He spoke in a tone of respect and awe.

"Excellent driving, sir."

## 8

One interesting thing about my line of work is that it never gets boring.

I wake up, have breakfast and start my day, just like anyone else. But then, a couple of hours later, I have imparted upon me the knowledge that I'm the target of contract killers.

Plus, my immediate future included a search for a handicapped drug dealer who goes by the nickname 'Wheels.' In the same general area my sister may or may not be.

Like I said, never a dull moment.

After my visit to Hammerhead, I drove home and went into a private room where I have my armory.

Even though it was a touch warm for jeans, I put on a pair so I could strap my Ruger .357 light carry revolver to my ankle.

In a holster at the back of my jeans, covered by a loose-fitting Hawaiian shirt went a custom-made Walther .45 ACP with a threaded barrel. Threaded, of course, for a sound suppressor.

Then, into the front pocket of my jeans, I slipped a very

compact silencer. An extra 12-round magazine went into the other pocket.

Maybe it was overkill, pun intended, but I knew the caliber (again, pun intended) of some of the men who might be coming after me. If there was any truth to what Hammerhead told me, I would much rather be over-equipped than to come up short. In my line of work, you're allowed to come up short once. And then it's all over.

Back in the Maverick, I cruised up Federal Highway – the road that travels parallel to I-95, and listened to the Rolling Stones in their countrified version of *Honky Tonk Women.*

*Country Honk.*

I've always been a fan of Keith Richards and I pictured him sitting in a bar, tipplin' a jar in Jackson.

Keith would love Florida.

Like just about everywhere in Southeast Florida, the action is always at the beach or near the beach.

Most of the bars and restaurants and the parties where illicit drug deals take place, are nine times out of ten at the beach.

Why?

Easy. Cops don't patrol the beach like they do the streets. If you're going to sell drugs, would you rather be in a drug-filled neighborhood crawling with cops on the prowl at all times, maybe even undercover? Or would you prefer to be down at the beach where people are spread out, drinking, getting high and generally having a good time?

Not to mention, drug dealers are just as vain as the rest of us. They like to stay tanned, check out the hard bodies at the beach, especially the oftentimes large, pendulous breasts barely contained by a thin strand of polyester purchased at a Bells outlet store.

And don't get me started on the thongs. There's a large segment of the beach-going population who apparently have no idea regarding the rules of thong wearing.

Some women are utterly unaware that they might have the kind of ass that doesn't merit a thong. And men? Please. No man in his right mind should wear a thong, or even a European speedo.

Then again, with either gender, you have to appreciate the confidence.

So, naturally, I headed for the beach, exiting at Boynton Beach Boulevard.

I followed that up and over the bridge that spanned the intercoastal, and followed it down to the A1A and the beach.

The A1A, or Ocean Boulevard as a lot of people think of it, runs right along the ocean where there is plenty of street parking. But even those spots fill up fast, especially during the peak season when the snowbirds have descended into Florida from their wintry climes. To accommodate the overflow, there are public parking lots on the other side of the A1A. Again, during peak season, those fill up awfully fast, too.

The issue became for me that if Wheels was indeed middle-management, he probably wouldn't be on the beach. His street-level dealers would be working the area, which led to the question of how I was going to find the specific dealers who could lead me to Wheels?

Plus, it would require just the right dealer.

Someone without confidence. Maybe someone who's still using themselves. I slowly made my way along the beach stopping to chat with people who looked like they were in the midst of partying. I casually struck up a couple of conversations, but didn't achieve any information. I worked several groups but most of them were suspicious, which made perfect sense. I didn't look like your average beachgoer.

But there's always one guy on the beach usually in his thirties or forties who looks at least a couple decades older. He'll be on a beat-up towel with a piece-of-shit guitar and a little bucket to panhandle for money, drugs or both.

Just the man I was looking for appeared about a mile up the beach from where I parked. He looked like Willie Nelson gone to seed.

I realize that's redundant.

He had a long greasy ponytail and brown skin that looked like a catcher's mitt that had taken a couple decades of ninety-mile-per-hour fastballs.

His guitar was truly a piece of garbage, he'd probably trash-picked it.

Instead of the standard six strings, it looked like it had about three and a half.

He was using it more as a percussion instrument, slapping his withered hand against the wood body, seemingly incapable of actually playing any music.

As I walked by, I took one look and knew that he was on drugs and desperately looking for money to fund his next fix.

"Hey Willie," I said. "Let's hear a song."

"Any requests?" he asked. His voice sounded like his throat was coated with barnacles.

I sat down next to him so I didn't look as intimidating and pulled out a fifty-dollar bill.

His bloodshot eyes looked at the fifty and it was like a cartoon bubble floating above his head, filled with floating joints, pills, and booze.

He put down the guitar.

"I'm looking for a job," I said. This seemed like a better

idea than trying to pretend to be a junkie. "Word on the street is that Wheels is hiring security."

He sort of jolted a little bit. The idea of a guy like me working security scared him. The only reason he was still there was the fifty-dollar bill. His eyes looked everywhere around me, but avoided direct contact. A guy walked past us dragging a kiteboard.

"I don't know, man," he said.

"Are you sure you don't know?"

"I don't know no Wheels," he said.

I pulled out another fifty and this time he looked so excited he was about to piss himself. He smelled like he already had.

"Look, I don't know this Wheels guy you're looking for," he whined. "I'm usually down around Pompano. I just came up here for the coin. Some of these dudes have serious cash, is what I heard."

"There's a lot floating around," I said. "If you know where to look." I waved the bills in front of him so he could actually smell it.

"A buddy of mine down in Pompano told me to hit up this chick," he said, licking his lips and not taking his eyes off the money. "She supposedly runs some product out of Silver Moon but like I said, I'm a low-level guy. Maybe she works for this Wheels guy you're looking for. I really don't know, man."

"What's her name?"

He held out his hand for the two fifties. I looked at him and waited. He worked up the courage to look me in the eye. Finally, he was able to will himself to speak.

"Sugar."

I refused to believe it.

Sure, there were dozens of women with the nickname 'Sugar' in Southeast Florida. Hell, there were probably a few dozen strippers with that nickname.

'Sugar' was also slang for several kinds of drugs, and a general term for much more.

Cocaine. Heroin. Sex.

*Give me some sugar.*

That could have a lot of meanings.

Still it was a good thing, the way I saw it.

The drug dealer I had put out of commission a while back told me my sister's nickname was Sugar and she was in Boynton Beach.

Which worked out perfectly because the case Dominique had hired me for was also apparently centered around Boynton Beach, and a boat named Brown Sugar.

*Kill two birds with one .45.*

Willie Nelson had told me Sugar pushed her drugs out of 'Silver Moon.' By that, he meant the Silver Moon Arcade, a funky establishment full of vintage games in downtown Delray Beach.

Back in the Maverick, I took the A1A to Atlantic Avenue, turned left and crossed the bridge over the intercoastal and cruised into downtown Delray Beach.

Like always it was packed.

A mixture of tourists, snowbirds, hipsters, retired folks and the occasional drug dealer thrown in. You always got the sense when you're walking around Delray Beach that it was like a beach town on steroids.

There were fancy expensive stores where you could buy a bikini for three hundred bucks, followed by a pizza place with the big roaring wood-burning oven in the middle of the dining room. There were cocktail bars, taco shops, ice cream parlors and a never-ending parade of vehicles. Everything from glorified golf carts equipped with turn signals to Bentley convertibles with New York plates to Harley-Davidson motorcycles and rusted out twenty-year-old Toyotas.

I-95 was the corridor that ran along the East Coast of the U.S., so a lot of the seasonal population of Delray Beach was from New York and New Jersey. It was not uncommon to see half of the vehicles in downtown Delray Beach sporting those states' plates.

Silver Moon Arcade was on Fourth Street so I turned right off of Atlantic, waited for a homeless guy with a shopping cart full of recyclables, and then parked in the arcade's little parking lot. I opened the door to an onslaught of noise. Bells ringing, pinball machine paddles slapping, video games emitting a series of incredibly loud and cacophonous whistles and bells.

Seconds later, I had a headache.

The place was much bigger on the inside that one would

expect. There had to be at least two hundred game machines, many of them I recognized from the eighties like Pac-Man and Donkey Kong.

There was a whole set of pinball machines from the fifties, sixties and seventies. I was almost tempted to play the Indiana Jones, Raiders of the Lost Ark pinball machine, but then I remembered why I was there.

Without a physical description and only a nickname, I had my work cut out for me. Luckily, I spotted what appeared to be the only employee in the place. He was very tall, probably 6'7" or 6'8" and couldn't have weighed more than 130 pounds or so.

On top of his thin frame was a giant mop of curly black hair. His skin was dark, probably of Caribbean descent and he had pale green eyes. I approached him and said, "Hey, man. You know if Sugar is around?"

"What are you, the fuzz?" he asked. Apparently since the arcade was retro the employees were asked to speak in retro language.

I kinda liked it. "Nope," I said. "But I really to hook up if you know what I mean." I started to rub my arm and fidgeted like I was in need of some drugs.

"Well, you're out of luck. Sugar don't come around here no more."

It sounded like a Van Morrison song.

"Why not?

"Man, this is an arcade. We're selling entertainment. An escape into the past. We're selling childhood memories. You dig?"

I dug.

"We don't need somebody else in here selling crap that competes with us. We want them to escape here, not here," he said, patting the vein on the inside of his arm. "You get what I mean, bro?"

"Sure do."

He looked at me, seemed to appreciate that I was going to drop it.

"If you're really jonesing, word on the street is that Sugar's moved up to West Palm. A little more disposable income up there. Place called Crush."

I took out one of my business cards. They were made of thick white stock with only my last name Carver and my cell phone. I pushed it across the top of the pinball machine next to us. It was a Charlie's Angels theme.

Everyone had loved Farrah Fawcett, but not me. I had serious lust for Jaclyn Smith. Those brunettes are dynamite.

"If Sugar does come back, can you have her give me a call?" I asked.

The tall, skinny dude's long face went sour like he'd just bitten into a rotten papaya.

"Man, who the hell are you?"

I pointed at the card.

"The name's Carver."

He rolled his eyes.

"What? I asked.

"You never met Sugar, have you? Why are you pretending?"

"Let's just say when I've met her, I've never been very aware, okay?"

"You must've been really messed up," he said.

"Why's that?"

The tall guy looked at me.

"Sugar isn't a she," he said. "Sugar's a he."

T hey called her the Goth Girl.

Or oftentimes it was just shortened to the Goth.

In rare cases, G.G., pronounced Gigi.

From where she came, no one knew. At some point, though, she landed in Florida. Fort Lauderdale, to be exact.

At the age of fifteen, she claimed to be eighteen to the owner of a strip club just off of I-95. She was slightly taller than average, with an athletic build and unnaturally large breasts for a girl with her frame.

In her line of work, it was the trifecta: youthful appearance, big boobs, and a slender body.

Needless to say, in a very short amount of time she made a very large sum of money. In cash.

One night a professional athlete was in the strip club. A "baller" as the girls liked to call them. Ballers tended to be big spenders, second only to rappers.

This particular baller had become enamored with her after a series of lap dances in the champagne room that totaled over two thousand dollars. He had asked for extra favors but she had refused. He begged her to go out with him but she said she didn't meet 'clients' outside of the club.

Having failed, he turned to straight up cash offers. He discovered she was done with work at two in the morning. After that, he said, if she spent the night with him he would give her ten thousand dollars in cash.

She declined and when the offer jumped to fifteen thousand, she declined again. It wasn't until the proposal of twenty-four thousand dollars for twenty-four hours of work was extended, that she accepted.

It was her entree into the world of being a high-end escort. And she quickly realized that her high earnings as a stripper had been strictly minor league.

Now, she was a true pro.

Over the course of eighteen months she became the call girl of choice for professional athletes in the greater Miami area and raked in nearly three million dollars in cash, jewelry, real estate, cars and miscellaneous gifts.

And then one night a defensive lineman for the Miami Dolphins started to treat her rough. He was an all-pro, signed to a huge contract the previous year, with an enormous signing bonus. The only thing bigger than his paycheck was his ego. And a supreme sense of entitlement. With everything, and everyone.

Especially with an escort.

She tried to get him to stop. In all the polite, semi-flirtatious ways. But he refused. He was a violent man, used to getting his way. She could see there would be no negotiation. He intended to hurt her. Badly.

So she stopped being polite.

The problem with really large and brutally strong people is that they assumed their size and strength were all they needed. But the owner of the strip club had been a serious practitioner of mixed martial arts including Krav Maga, silat, jujitsu and even a little kung fu. He had been especially fond of joint manipulation. The Goth Girl had spent a lot of time training with him. At first, it had been a basic course in self-defense. Something the owner offered to especially young strippers. After awhile, though, she became obsessed with it. And it wasn't long before she was more skilled than her teacher. After that, she went and sought new instructors, with more skills and tactics.

So when the giant lineman decided to hurt her, the first thing she did was pop the big man's elbow joint. It took all her strength but it happened so fast he didn't know what had transpired.

However the pain was intense and his face filled with rage.

With one arm hanging uselessly by his side, he bull rushed her.

Which is when he made his second mistake. She easily slid to the floor, tripped him and caught his other arm on the way down, and dislocated his shoulder by twisting it and torquing her body.

She sprang to her feet as he screamed in pain and pushed himself up to his knees. She grabbed a trophy off the mantle above the bedroom's fireplace and her eyes caught the wording on the plaque.

It said NFL's Humanitarian Award – Man of the Year.

She walked back over, raised the trophy above her head and smashed it into the back of his skull.

Much later, she found out that he had survived a severe skull fracture but never played another down in the NFL.

Not only was his career as an athlete finished, but her livelihood as an escort was over, too. Word got out about the

Goth Girl among the ballers and rappers, and her days of escort service were over.

However, as the saying goes, when one door closes, another one opens.

Miami was full of people who realized they could use a sexy, smart and dangerous woman who knew how to mete out some serious punishment.

That's how the Goth Girl met Mr. Springs, a tanned white man wearing a thousand dollar suit and a twenty thousand dollar watch.

He set up a meeting in a public place and explained, vaguely, what he did. That he was a liaison for certain organizations. These were groups of men who needed things done, always secretly and under the radar.

He offered her a job. A trial of sorts.

The fee wasn't huge because she needed to prove herself first, he claimed. If the first job went fine there would be more to come at higher rates. He also made it clear that if the first job was a failure, the penalty would be severe.

Ultimately, it was a clear success. Almost effortless.

After being a stripper, and then an escort, the Goth Girl had found her true calling.

In less than two years, she became one of Miami's highest paid assassins.

## 11

P alm Beach.

Old money, Donald Trump and The Breakers.

Across from Palm Beach, over the intercoastal, was West Palm Beach.

Sort of like Palm Beach's little brother who never quite lived up to his potential. Entry point for real estate in Palm Beach was probably around four million or so, for a tiny home in the least desirable of locations.

In West Palm Beach, just a half-mile away, four million was close to the high water mark. And that would buy you a big home with water views.

While there are really no bad neighborhoods in Palm Beach as it's all one giant ode to American capitalism and excess, West Palm has ghettos, strip malls and crime.

From I-95 I cruised into downtown West Palm where I was met with a funky little section of shops, restaurants and a public park where concerts are held in the summer. The area faces the intercoastal and the mansions beyond.

The guy from the Silver Moon Arcade told me if I was

really desperate to use, I might be able to find Sugar at a place called Crush.

I found a parking spot a few blocks down from the place, went inside and discovered a dive bar that looked like some kind of a refugee from the nineties. In fact, it had the appearance of an establishment that had gone through dozens of incarnations and had somehow amassed a few qualities from each.

The present version of Crush was sort of a mix between a Mexican restaurant and a singles bar from circa 1992. The floor was dark wood, the walls painted blood red, and here and there were skulls watching the disinterested customers eating uninspired food and getting sloshed.

By now it was early evening so I ordered a bottle of Pacifico from a young waitress with a nose ring. Unfortunate, because she would have been pretty without the hardware sticking out of her nostril.

I had stopped along the way at the bank and withdrew some cash for bribes. I would provide receipts to Dominique and hopefully she would reimburse me. If not, I could write it off as a business expense. I put a fifty between my fingers.

"Have you seen Sugar around?"

She looked at me like I'd grabbed her ass.

"No foreplay?" she asked.

"You're busy, otherwise I would have taken it slow," I answered.

"How about ordering an appetizer so I've got time to think about if I want to answer that question."

"Will guacamole give you enough time?" I said. "And if not, throw in a couple of carnitas."

She left and I nursed the Pacifico, looked around at the other clientele. Pretty sad state of affairs. It looked like there were a few tourists who had lost their way. I was fairly certain Crush hadn't received a rave review from Fodors.

There was a table of construction workers, a couple of women who looked like they worked in an office and either left early or never went back after lunch. And then the requisite beach bums at the bar. They would probably be the ones buying drugs. Although you never knew, the tourists might be in to get some nose candy for the beach or for later tonight.

The girl brought me the guac and set it down on the table.

"Order another Pacifico and I'll probably have an answer for you," she said.

"Another Pacifico and an answer sound great to me," I said and then tried the guacamole. It was perhaps the worst I'd ever tasted. It was more like avocado-flavored toothpaste.

Nose Ring came back with my beer and said, "If he's not here, your best bet is the park. And if he's not there, I heard he has a place in Palm Towers."

She slid across another piece of paper. "I had a little extra time so I came up with this information, too."

She left and I glanced down at the piece of paper and what was written on it.

A phone number.

And my waitress's name.

Jalissa.

## 12

S ugar wasn't at the park.

That conclusion wasn't reached through any great detective work on my part, because there was no one at the park at all.

South Florida was home to plenty of rain and it looked like the day had become no exception. By the time I left Crush and got to the park, drizzle had started. It would be gone in probably half an hour and the sun would come out. The evening would be hot and steamy before the night's cooler breeze arrived.

So I pointed the Maverick toward Palm Towers.

I knew of Palm Towers but I had never actually been inside. It was a cool Art Deco-ish apartment building that had probably gone up in the seventies. It was a cylindrical column of white concrete and each unit had a semicircular balcony.

The building looked like a stack of oddly shaped dinner plates.

The more expensive units faced the intercoastal and could see Palm Beach and maybe even glimpse the ocean beyond. The cheap side of Palm Towers faced the freeway and looked over the unsightly sprawl of West Palm.

The views were night and day. The units facing the intercoastal would probably go for 400k or so. The ones facing I-95 would top out at 200k or so. Less, if they needed work.

I parked in a guest spot, locked up the Maverick and went inside through the front doors. There was a small vestibule and the main doors into the tower were locked.

Phone in hand, I waited about ten minutes for a resident to leave. I put the phone to my ear as if I was on a call and when the resident, a tan woman in shorts and a workout tank top with headphones came out, I got the door before it closed.

Once inside, I realized the problem was I didn't really have a good description of Sugar and didn't know which unit he was in. I walked past the elevators, turned left and saw that the doors led outside to the pool deck. I went through them to find a large circular pool that overlooked the intercoastal and the seawall.

There were a couple of older folks sitting around the pool but I knew they wouldn't have the information I needed. There was a slightly younger man on the seawall, fishing. I walked over to him, glanced over the ledge and saw there was about an eight-foot drop.

The current was strong here and there were no boats passing by.

"Catching anything?" I asked.

"Nope. That's why they call it fishing and not catching."

I had a comedian here. He was a little older than I first thought, probably in his late thirties or forties. He had on a Grateful Dead T-shirt along with a wannabe Indiana Jones fedora. He really couldn't pull the look off though, thanks to his thick legs and fat feet stuffed into some worn out Birkenstocks.

"Hey, I was supposed to pick up my buddy Sugar," I said. "I was just at Crush and he wasn't there, either."

The name drop was a way of implying that I was a druggie.

He barely glanced at me.

"Best not to mention that name around here," the guy said with a snickering laugh and a backward glance at the old folks around the pool. "He's not the most popular resident here, they've been trying to get rid of him for years."

It made sense to me. Drug dealers don't tend to be the most popular people in their neighborhoods.

"Well, he's not answering his cell," I offered, even though I didn't know the number.

The guy glanced up over my head and I followed his gaze. He seemed to be looking at the balcony about three floors up.

"He's probably still sleeping. Because if he isn't, he's usually sitting out there."

"Yep, that's Sugar all right," I added.

"If I see him, I'll tell him you were here. What's your name?"

"Babe Winkelman."

"Cool name. Okay, I'll let him know, Babe."

"Thanks and there's a sale at Publix right now on mahi-mahi. I think that's the only way you're gonna get fish for dinner."

"You're probably right," he said with a defeatist attitude.

"You gotta be more confident than that," I said. "Fish can sense a lack of confidence."

Back inside, I went to the elevator and took it to the third floor. Once in the hallway, I oriented myself to the corner that would overlook the intercoastal.

Satisfied I was facing the right way, I walked down to the last unit on the left and knocked on the door.

There was no answer.

I waited and knocked again.

No answer.

I listened for a cell phone ringing just in case my fisherman friend decided to warn Sugar that an unpleasant-looking man might be stopping by but I heard no cell phone ringing and it was now decision time.

If I broke in and it wasn't Sugar's condo I might have some explaining to do. My fishing buddy's glance could just have easily been at the fifth floor or even the second floor.

I might be barging in on a couple of 80-year-olds taking their after-dinner nap at this hour. Or worse, testing out a new bottle of Viagra.

I decided to risk it and slid out my lock picking tool from my belt. I jimmied the lock and it slid open. I stepped into the condo and knew instantly I had the right place. It stunk of weed, along with the coppery scent of blood.

Once inside, I saw someone had spilled Sugar all over the floor.

The man formally known as Sugar was sprawled out in the middle of the floor, obviously quite dead.

I knew this because his head was mostly detached from his body and his neck had been shredded.

There was blood everywhere and oddly enough, it looked to me like there were tire tracks.

Right across what was left of Sugar's throat.

## 13

W*heels.*

At first I thought maybe the tracks were footprints.

As if someone had stepped on this throat and then walked away. But the tracks were too thin and uniform.

Plus, they looked like they held a tread pattern but not like any kind I'd seen before. There were tiny little marks and scratches here and there. When I compared them to Sugar's throat, it made me wonder if they were tire chains.

It seemed weird, but this was Florida. There's no stranger place in the world than southeast Florida.

Back to Sugar. Gazing down, I could tell he was a big dude, easily tipping the scales at 270 or 280. He had wild hair, a thick beard and a tattoo along his arm that read 'Sugar.' He was dressed in the usual gear: sweatpants, a T-shirt and one flip flop. The other one was a few feet away.

Looking around the condo, it was about what you'd expect from a drug dealer's place of residence. A lot of big, overstuffed furniture well-worn from people who wanted to lounge after getting high.

Everything smelled of weed, body odor and fried food.

I wondered if Sugar was Cuban because I was fairly sure some of the odor could be Mofongo, the Cuban dish of mashed plantains.

It appeared to me that someone had officially terminated one of Boynton Beach's street dealers. Maybe it had been his boss, Wheels. Maybe Sugar had been skimming the profits, or indulging in the product himself.

Whatever the reason, the solution had been permanent.

All that was left to do was search the place quickly and get the hell out. Just in case my fishing buddy was the paranoid sort and had already called the cops.

The place consisted of a kitchen and living room, two bedrooms and two bathrooms. I took a quick peek out onto the deck that overlooked the intercoastal. I saw no trace of anything important, including Sugar's phone. No mail was laying around either, but I didn't expect to find a drug dealer like Sugar to have a whole lot of paperwork.

I didn't bother concerning myself with drugs and/or cash. The party responsible for the murder had certainly taken care of all that. But they would not necessarily be looking for the same kinds of things I was looking for.

Namely, information.

I knew that anything electronic would be gone. Computers, laptops, iPads and phones. In fact, I saw more than a few chargers with nothing to connect to.

Sugar's keys were gone too and I assumed his car was with its new owner.

I was about to leave quietly, making sure to wipe down anything I'd touched to remove fingerprints. It would be in my best interest to slip out without anyone seeing me so that if I was eventually questioned, I could just say I knocked, but couldn't get in.

And then I stopped. There was one place I hadn't really checked. Every kitchen has a little drawer where everyone throws their crap from the kitchen counter, just before company arrives.

The junk drawer. Which takes on a double meaning in a drug dealer's home.

Not that Sugar was ever too worried about appearances. Certainly physical appearances, judging by what I could see rolled out in the middle of the floor. I found the drawer next to the refrigerator and inside there were twist ties, pens, rubber bands, paperclips, a couple of pens, half of a cookie, and a wine cork.

There were also a few crumbled receipts and some loose change.

I took out the receipts, unfolded them and smoothed them out.

There was one from Crush, but then the rest of the receipts were from a strip club in West Palm called Rebecca's.

I've heard of it but had never been there.

Honestly.

I checked the clock and saw that by now it was after seven and the light had started to fade.

It was the perfect time to grab a beer at Rebecca's and see what I could find.

## 14

Y ou've seen one strip club you've seen them all.

Oh sure, you've got your small differences. The level of gaudiness on the façade in front of the low-rent building. Some cheap decoration to justify an Arabian name, or an exotic theme.

Once inside, you're treated to the watered-down drinks and the hiked-up skirts of the servers.

The percentage of dancers who are actually drug addicts, doing what they have to do to get their next score, is as high as they are.

Totally nude is where no alcohol can be served. Partially nude means a full and active liquor license. The difference between the two places is usually an indication of the customer's relationship with alcohol.

Some guys are there for the bare asses.

Some guys are there for the Bud Lights, with a little eye candy on the side.

There is some leeway in terms of groping the naked drug addicts. Rebecca's was somewhere in the middle.

The dancers wore thongs which meant there was plenty of booze flowing.

Private lap dances happened behind a door to the left of the stage.

There were no expensive champagne rooms which meant the place rarely had high rollers in attendance. It was a middle-of-the-road strip club for middle-aged men. Probably of middle-class means.

The fact that Sugar was a dealer here meant that he was supplying the dancers, not the customers.

It was a little bit early so it wasn't too crowded. There was one dancer on the stage who looked like she could've played middle linebacker on a Division III football team. It would take a brave soul to buy a lap dance with her.

There was a female bartender who clearly had been a dancer twenty years ago. Or maybe it hadn't been that long but a drug addiction could have aged her. It also might have prevented her from getting a real job and forced her to be in the club watching young women go through the same gauntlet that had chewed her up and spat her out like a piece of gnawed meat stuck in the windpipe.

There was another dancer sitting at the bar smoking a cigarette who glanced at me sideways as I took a seat and ordered a beer.

There were about twenty other people in the club scattered about at tables or in the high-backed booths. The cushioned upholstery was covered with the requisite red velvet and probably stank of cigarette smoke, body sweat and desperation.

Most of the customers were solitary men, naturally, and I saw two couples who were probably looking to spice up their relationship with a little 'naughty' fun.

A pair of young women were sitting alone at the bar. I

pegged them as dancers having a drink either before or after their shift. Probably before. If I worked here, as soon as I was done I would get the hell out.

When the bartender put my beer in front of me, I slipped her a twenty and told her to keep the change.

"Let everyone know Sugar can't make it tonight, but that I'm here in his place. As his representative."

The woman looked at me with a complete lack of emotion and pocketed the twenty with the same dead expression.

The skinny chick at the end of the bar picked up her drink which I was sure was cranberry juice. She put out her cigarette, after all she had no way of knowing if the client she was about to lay her sales pitch onto was a smoker or not. Some guys hated the smell of cigarettes and I included myself in that category.

She came up and used the age-old line: "Is this seat taken?" She pointed a skinny finger with a long fake nail at the bar stool next to me.

"It is now," I said, using the standard response.

She smiled, sat down and to save her from making the pitch I said to her, "Just so you know, I'm here for Sugar. He's incapacitated at the moment."

She gave a little smirk when she realized I wasn't going to be a paying customer and fished out a cigarette.

"You mind?" She inclined her head toward the cigarette.

"Only if you give me some information," I said.

She shook her head.

"Sugar didn't send you," she said.

"Why do you say that?"

She fired up her cigarette and turned to face me. Very young. Barely eighteen, but they had been eighteen very hard years.

When she smoked, I could see her teeth were crooked and yellow, already coated with a lifetime of nicotine.

Her voice was raspy.

She blew out a stream of smoke and answered my question.

"Because Sugar is dead."

"Carlie, get your scrawny ass up on the back stage, bitch," a man said.

From behind her, a man cuffed the stripper in the back of the head. Her face turned red and the drink in her hand spilled on the bar. Her jaw set and I could see the anger on her face. But she bit it back, like she had for a long, long time.

I glanced behind her at the man who'd hit her. He was a big, beefy dude with tattoos down both thick arms. He was probably 6'4" and well over three hundred pounds. Probably closer to three-fifty. Maybe even four.

"She's with me," I said.

He squinted at me like I was a fly about to land on his plate of pork chops.

"I don't see any money changing hands," he said. "Plus, you can go find a real woman not this skinny piece of tail. Hell, I'd screw a piece of plywood before her." He went to cuff her up against the head again but I was a tad quicker and I caught his left hand, grabbed his pinky finger and squeezed it from its base to the tip until the middle knuckle shattered.

It made a little popping sound like a silencer on a .22 Magnum.

He gritted his teeth and the stripper, Carlie, looked at me like I was insane.

The bouncer growled at me. "You. Outside. Right now."

I slipped a fifty-dollar bill into the skinny stripper's hand along with one of my business cards.

The bartender was probably already calling the cops so I walked quickly past the stage, the tables by the door, and outside. As soon as I cleared the main doors I heard just the slightest shuffle of feet behind me and I knew the big side of beef was already throwing his first punch.

I ducked and did a rear kick into his midsection. It was like kicking a school bus.

His enormous ham fist whizzed right over my head. I spun around and unleashed an uppercut all the way from the South side, as they say. It smashed him in the face and half of his teeth folded back into his mouth. He stood, swaying, and I threw a right hook that landed on the button and he crashed to the ground, landing on his back. His head slammed into the pavement with a hard, wet sound. If my punch hadn't turned out the lights, the ground certainly had finished the job.

Immediately, I heard the shifting of gravel behind me and I turned just in time to see two men closing in on me.

Hammerhead's words echoed in my brain.

*There's a contract out on you.*

One had a knife, the other had a gun. But I instinctively knew the gun was just security. They wanted to kill me quietly and were hoping the one with the knife could get the job done. If he couldn't, the man with the gun would have to step in and finish me.

It turned out, neither one was up to the task.

The knife man had chosen the right angle of attack, but his speed was all wrong. He was being a little too careful and aimed the knife instead of going for a general area with speed and power.

I was able to slap the knife to the side when he came close. The point of the blade cut through my shirt and raked my side, so the guy wasn't that slow. A quarter-second faster and it might have gotten home.

I stepped in with my right hand and got him by the throat. He was a small, agile little guy. Wiry and tough. Dark-skinned and very short. Either Mexican, or maybe Guatemalan.

But with my left hand clamped onto his right, I squeezed until his bones started cracking and then my right hand squeezed as well, crushing his trachea.

Pushing him backward, we crashed into his colleague who was trying to step around us to get a clean shot.

He never made it.

We all went down in a heap with me on top.

I reached around the first man and got my hand on the gun. It fired a wild shot.

For better leverage, I rotated my body and used my weight to pin down both of my smaller attackers. I momentarily let go of the guy who had wielded the knife and got both hands on the gun.

I wrenched it free and put the muzzle into the first man's chest and fired six times, hoping the caliber of bullet was strong enough to go through the first body and into the second.

It was.

The first man was clearly dead, and the second needed a final bullet in the forehead.

The bodyguard was dead, too. The wild bullet must not have been so wild, after all.

I wiped the gun down and put it in the knife man's hand. A shoot-out between two men and the bouncer of the club.

A quick glance told me there were no security cameras out front.

I was glad.

They say the camera adds ten pounds.

## 16

T he pool surface looked like a clear sheet of jade.

I slipped into the water and casually swam laps with no real thoughts on my mind. The scratch I'd received from the attacker with the knife was just that, a scratch. Swimming didn't open the wound so I wasn't worried about it. Plus, I had pocketed the knife and tossed it out the car window so my DNA wouldn't be at the crime scene.

It didn't bother me at all that I had killed two men. Especially those two. Contract killers. Coming after me made it clear they had no morals when it came to accepting a job. They probably killed women and children, too.

As far as I was concerned, I'd relieved the world of two dangerous parasites.

The only real drawback was that potentially people would remember me from the club. Describe me to the cops who had certainly arrived.

I had a good friend, Paula Barbieri, on the Delray Beach police force. She would possibly give me a heads up if my name came up.

Then again, she might not.

The fisherman had seen me at Sugar's condo. And there had been plenty of witnesses at the strip club, but they only saw me walk outside with the bouncer. The scene I'd left had told a complete story, without including me. Plus, I was fairly confident the young stripper with bad teeth wouldn't offer my business card. She seemed to know when to keep information to herself.

So, for now I figured I was okay.

I got out of the pool and even though Florida is known for its heat, there was an evening chill in the air. After toweling off, I went inside, locked up the house, set the alarm, and poured myself two fingers of fairly good whiskey.

The state of my current investigation did not bring me joy.

I was no closer to finding Wheels and no closer to finding the boat Dominique had hired me to locate.

Worst of all, I had no idea of my next steps. The level of whiskey slowly sank to zero so I refilled my glass and sat down again just as my cell phone dinged with a text message.

I glanced down and read the words on the screen.

*2210 HORSE HEAVEN. Palm Beach.*
*Sugar's boss.*
*Be careful.*
*-C.*

IT TOOK me a second to figure out the sender's identity.

The stripper.

*Carlie.*

## 17

Pretentious people get on my nerves.

For instance, the ones who have to name their houses. Oh, I don't mind it when "normal" folks like you and I do it. In that case, it's a certain hominess. And friendliness. Usually, a cottage we want to get away to for the weekend so we call it Camp Relax, or something.

No, that doesn't bother me.

What chafes my marble sack are the mega millionaires who feel the need to call their mega mansions pretentious-ass names like "Cherry Blossom." Or "Island Palace."

Yeah, vomit-worthy in my opinion.

It's almost as if they're so full of themselves that they can't have a street address like "ordinary" people. Like it's an insult when they've invested twenty million dollars into a home they can't simply refer to it as 334 West Maple.

No.

For instance, "Horse Heaven." In Palm Beach. A bastion of wealth and fame.

I did have to smile at the name, though.

Horse Heaven.

It told me that Carlie might actually have been telling me the truth, that the house belonged to Sugar's drug boss.

Horse, after all, is slang for something Sugar was ultimately involved in.

*Heroin.*

## 18

The next morning, after breakfast of pancakes made with oat bran, my cell phone buzzed.

It was my new boss.

Dominique.

"Good morning," she said.

"What's good about it?" Everything was good about it, actually. I had a nice breakfast, and I was about to go ruin some rich guy's day in Palm Beach, at his big house with the pretentious name. But I couldn't say that to Dominique. I had to act gruff, for some reason. Make it sound like this was hard work and I wasn't necessarily enjoying it, which, of course, I was.

"Aren't you just a ray of sunshine?" she pointed out.

"No, you're the sunshine," I said. "I'm the sunblock. SPF 90."

It was difficult for me to talk to Dominique and not imagine her body. Ebony skin, taut muscles, a figure that belonged on both a model and an athlete. A model athlete.

"Update, please," she said.

"I've got a line on the boat. It might be in Palm Beach."

Yeah, it was a bit of a lie. The lead on my sister was in Palm Beach, tied to a drug dealer named Wheels. But I figured I could look up there for the boat. After all, my initial online search had turned up the name Joaquin Villabosa, a flamboyant resident of Palm Beach.

I figured when I was up looking for Horse Heaven, I might able to get a lead on Brown Sugar.

It was all about efficiencies.

"That wouldn't surprise me," Dominique said, which naturally surprised the hell out of me.

"Why do you say that?"

"Let's just say my client has a lot of golfing buddies up in Palm Beach."

I'd heard that a lot of the PGA guys like Tiger Woods and Dustin Johnson, who usually hang out in Jupiter, sometimes come down to Palm Beach for golf and better parties.

Word was, they got pretty wild. Single guys, famous, with tons of money have been known to attract all kinds of attention, beyond the female kind. Who knows, maybe some of them liked to hang out with Joaquin Villabosa. And maybe they bought drugs from a guy named Wheels.

That would be too good to be true. Still, it was a small world. And the Palm Beach community was extremely incestuous. Figuratively and literally.

"What's the lead?" she asked.

"I can't say right now, other than it's from one of my sources."

"Okay, keep me posted."

She hung up abruptly and before I put down the phone, I sent Carlie a message.

*"Why did you say Sugar was dead?"*

I hadn't had a chance to follow up with her when she'd

casually mentioned it. A giant Neanderthal had gotten in the way.

No better time than the present, so I put a gun in my ankle holster, threw on a shoulder holster and filled it with a .45. A linen sport coat, teal, of course, over jeans and suede shoes with no socks made me feel like a true Palm Beacher.

The Maverick wasn't going to fit in, unless someone thought I was an aged venture capitalist, trying to relive his youth.

A quick cruise down Atlantic Avenue took me to I-95 and I followed that to Palm Beach. Once over the intercoastal, I slowed and cruised the streets.

It wasn't until a half hour later that I cruised past a mansion that had an iron gate. On one side, was the silhouette of a horse, rising up and pawing at the air.

On the other, was a silhouette of clouds, with sun rays bursting from behind them.

*Horse Heaven.*

## 19

There's no real way to establish a stakeout in Palm Beach. First, no one parks on the street. Second, it's eerily quiet. Not many pedestrians. Very little vehicular traffic.

The other problem is that if you don't look like you either own a twenty-million-dollar mansion, or work at one, it's obvious. Now, if I had unlimited funds, I would rent a house somewhere nearby and set up there. Get some cameras, maybe a set of binoculars, and stock up on good food for a real, genuine stakeout.

But I wasn't about to ask Dominique for twenty-five grand to rent a Palm Beach house for a few days.

So, I did the only thing possible, which was to circle around in regular intervals. I took different routes and tried to spread them out as much as possible. I stopped a couple of times to fill the tank up.

It wasn't until about my twelfth circuit around Palm Beach that activity occurred at Horse Heaven. I had passed the house and was about to turn onto a cross street when I saw, in my rearview mirror, the gates to the big house open and a Bentley pulled out.

It was perfect timing.

Pushing the pedal to the floor, I roared down the cross street, made a hard right and sped down the road, making a parallel path to the Bentley. When I turned right, I saw its taillights up ahead.

Now, the challenge went from staking someone out to tailing them. A much easier proposition, even with a car as unique as mine.

The Bentley was dark green, with big-ass back tires. Probably a GT. A couple hundred thousand to try to impress your Palm Beach neighbors, and fail. No one was impressed with anything here.

The Bentley turned left and headed out of Palm Beach proper, into West Palm and somehow, I knew where they were going.

An airport. These guys wouldn't fly commercial, and there was a small airport for private planes just north of the main airport. It was very private and exclusive.

I cursed under my breath.

It all depended on where they might be going.

The Bentley pulled into the airport's entrance and disappeared inside. Probably a valet parking area.

It was desperation time. I had to get inside there, see who it was, and to what destination they might be flying.

There was a single-story building with a sign out front advertising granite and marble sales. I parked the Maverick in their parking lot and hurried back to the airport, hoping the car wouldn't get towed.

The airport had a little banner across the front door of the main building, reading Execu-Airport. It was like a long, low airplane hangar, probably had been one, originally.

Through the front glass doors I went, and found myself

in an open space with a lounge to the right, a pair of big, wide doors through which I could see a couple of small jets, and a front desk with a man in a blue suit watching me.

"Can I help you, sir?" he asked.

I was faced with what I call the three Bs: Bribe, Bullshit, Bodily Harm.

My first instinct was bodily harm. A little bit tricky, though, being at an airport. I'm sure someone, somewhere was armed. Too many unknowns.

Bribery wasn't a great option, either. There were rich guys here all the time. A few hundred bucks wasn't going to have a lot of pull.

So, I went with bullshit.

"Look, I'm supposed to surprise one of those guys with his lady friend, not his wife, in a limo at the airport where they're going. He lands, gets whisked into the limo where she's waiting for him wearing nothing but a bottle of Dom Perignon and a smile. Trouble is, I don't know what time they land. And I couldn't ask him, as his wife was in the way."

The guy smirked at my predicament, but didn't bat an eye at the story. He glanced down and tapped a screen in front of him.

He looked back up at me.

Sometimes, it takes more than one "B."

I pulled out five one-hundred-dollar bills and slid them across to him.

It was worth it. Because when I'd glanced out at the runway where a private jet was sitting, I saw the passengers from the Bentley headed toward it.

One of them was in a wheelchair.

The man in the blue suit, after taking my money, gave me the information quietly, and under his breath.

"Let's see, FPO, 7:34 p.m. arrival."

FPO.

Freeport.

*The Bahamas.*

ack outside, I stood in a little bit of a daze. The information had been nothing special. So what? A rich drug dealer in a wheelchair was taking a private jet to the Bahamas. What's the big deal? Happens all the time. A lot of stuff goes on in the Bahamas. Much easier to bribe cops over there.

Plus, from the east coast of Florida, a fast boat can get there in two hours. Maybe even less.

Still, the idea of the Bahamas, and Freeport especially had triggered something in me. As I stood there, I felt like it was slipping away. I tried to picture it in my mind. And that word, 'picture' suddenly sent my mind flying backward in a blurry flashback to my initial online search for Joaquin Villabosa. The pictures I'd seen of the rich guy with this fancy homes, cars and his winery. The boat, Brown Sugar, had been in one of the pictures. At the time, the image had puzzled me. Seemed familiar. A marina, for sure. With a flag, mostly aquamarine, and a sign reading "Pro."

Now, I knew.

It had been taken in Freeport.

## 21

My credit card took the hit for a flight to the Bahamas, and I hoped Dominique would reimburse me even though I didn't get pre-approval. I thought about texting her, but the plane was boarding and I didn't have time.

It was a quick flight and I used the time to think through my plan. I'd parked the Maverick in long-term, and left all of my weapons in the car. No way to get through airport security with them.

Which meant job number one would be to find myself some kind of weapon. Or, find someone with one and take it from them, which I chose as my first option. No paperwork involved in that scenario.

There wasn't even time for a drink from the plane's beverage service, so I landed in Freeport with nothing but my phone, wallet and some cash.

The first thing I did was grab a rental car and a map. I'd been to Freeport once before, but it had been years ago. It's not a big town, mostly a place for cruise ships to dump pale tourists with bulging pockets for a day or so.

The one time I'd been to Freeport had been on a case involving a runaway. Turned out, the kid hadn't run at all. He'd sailed to Freeport with a South Beach prostitute and his daddy's boat. They'd wound up in Lucaya, which is right next to Freeport, and were having a grand old time. The place they'd stopped was a small, private marina full of big, expensive boats.

That's where I'd recognized Villabosa's boat.

And that's where I headed now.

It was a straight shot from the airport to the south coast of the island, where the private marina was located. There was a gate, but as I cruised by, I saw that it was unattended.

Perfect.

Acting like I owned the place, I cruised into the marina, spotted an open parking spot near a giant yacht that was cradled in the air by a massive, portable hoist, and parked.

Near the base of the hoist, I saw a hard hat and a spool of discarded cable. I walked over, put on the hard hat, picked up the cable and began to walk the marina.

It wasn't huge.

The layout was simple. Three channels cut into the land, each one with a dozen yachts parked. Beyond the canals was a ring of huge storage buildings, large enough to house a fleet of mega yachts. To the right of the storage buildings was the repair and maintenance yard, complete with more of the huge, blue yacht hoists, as well as various fuel trucks, equipment haulers and welding rigs.

I started at the furthest channel, and walked with the spool of cable in one hand, and my phone in the other, as if I was on my way to a job site. I passed a few people, mostly other workers, who gave no pause as I passed them. I figured a shipyard like this was a fairly transient place. Independent contractors would come and go. The support staff would be the same, no doubt. Still, I was the kind of guy who didn't exactly invite conversation.

The first channel didn't house what I was looking for.

Neither did the second one.

However, in the third channel I found her.

Brown Sugar.

## 22

D ominique answered on the first ring.

"Carver," she said.

"I'm looking at Brown Sugar, and not the kind you sprinkle onto your oatmeal."

I had stepped back from the channel, and now stood by a pile of scrap metal. If anyone were to pass me by, maybe they would think I was appraising it for its value.

"Where?" she asked.

"The Bahamas. Freeport."

"You're in the Bahamas?" She sounded like she didn't believe me. Which kind of hurt my feelings.

"Yes, and I'm hoping you'll reimburse me the airfare," I said. "It was a hunch that turned out to be a pretty good idea."

There was a pause and it sounded like she set something down on a counter.

"Am I interrupting dinner?" I asked. I checked my watch.

"No," she said. "Well, sort of. Just leftovers."

"You're eating alone? What a shame."

Yes, I was flirting. No, nothing wrong with that at all.

"You need to get on board and see if the goods are inside," she said. "If the goods are there, I need you to bring it back to Florida."

I laughed at her.

"Are you crazy? Get inside? Bring it back?" I asked. "There's only one way to go on board and it's straight up a single walkway, in view of everyone. Plus, I have no idea who's on board. And stealing a boat that might be full of stolen goods is well beyond what you're paying me to do."

"I'll double your fee," she said.

"No way."

"Triple."

There's always a way, I thought. Plus, good things come in threes. I believe that applied to triples as well.

"Plus, you let me take you out to dinner," I said.

"There's always a way," she said.

I knew I had a connection with her. We even thought alike.

Just then, I heard someone behind me and then a horrible, stabbing pain shot into my neck and I felt my knees buckle.

My last thought as I sank to the ground was that I may have just found my way inside the boat.

## 23

"The contract is awake," a voice said.

I opened my eyes. I was flat on my back on the floor, my arms and legs bound together. And I had somehow been tied in place.

Even worse, my head was immobile. Something was strapped to my forehead, pulling it back, and I couldn't move.

My neck was totally exposed.

I immediately thought of Sugar, dead in his apartment.

A man stood before me. He had on torn blue jeans, a black leather jacket, sunglasses perched on top of his head, and a gun in his hand.

The weird thing was, I knew him.

His name was Drake and he was a hired gun. A hitman. Very well-known in Florida as a fixer for dirty politicians.

"Sorry about that stun gun, brother," he said to me. "But money's money, and someone wanted you pretty badly.

He gave me a quick half-salute. "I'd heard a lot about you. Kind of surprised you got caught talking on the phone."

Out of the corner of my eye I saw a woman leaning up against the wall. She was tall, dressed all in black. Very goth-looking. I couldn't get a good look at her, though. I assumed she was Drake's girlfriend. There for the fun.

A door banged open and I heard someone wheezing.

Two men appeared. One of them was in a wheelchair as he rolled into view.

"Hey shithead," he said.

"Hey there, Wheels," I said.

His face turned red. I guess it was one of those nicknames people use behind the owner's back.

"Fucker," he said. "Kick him."

Someone next to me drove a boot into my side. It hurt. But not too bad.

I looked at the other man.

"Villabosa."

He did a mock little bow. Mr. Flamboyant. Here on his own boat.

"Another one of Dominique's red shirts bites the dust," he said, referencing Star Trek. The red shirts were the anonymous crew members who were usually killed at the start of each episode. Disposable. Expendable.

Nothing surprised me much anymore.

"She's not a lawyer," Villabosa said to me. "She paid your buddy Hammerhead to drop the name Wheels so you'd come running."

It took me a minute, but I caught up.

"Dominque's your partner," I said.

"Ex-partner, who feels she has a share in all of this. Which she doesn't."

"Enough bullshit," Wheels said. "Put 'em on."

The guy who kicked me came into view. He was carrying

two circular rings of metal blades, which he fastened, carefully, to the wheelchair's tires.

It didn't take a genius to know what was going to happen.

I lunged upward but the restraints holding my head and feet in place held firm. Whatever was used to keep my arms in place, however, moved a little. Just enough to let me try a second time, putting all my effort into my arms. I've always been a tad stronger on my right side, and that was the restraint that gave.

With one arm free, I reached wildly and felt the leg of something. A table. Or a desk.

"Now!" someone yelled.

I heard the clickety-clack of the metal blades on the wheelchair's tires.

They were getting closer. I heaved on the table again and this time I saw a pair of black boots in front of my face. One of them came up just as something toppled off the table I was yanking on. Whatever it was, it landed on my face just as a boot came crashing down on my skull.

Just before everything went black one more time, I heard a series of popping noises.

It was either the capillaries in my brain bursting.

Or gunfire.

## 24

I was free.

Not as in, I'm dead and now floating up to heaven, free for all of eternity.

Free as in someone had untied me, and the black fog that had crashed into my skull was leaving quickly.

Things came into view.

A wheelchair tipped on its side, a pool of blood leading from underneath it.

Drake, also on the floor, a bullet hole in the middle of his forehead.

Joaquin Villabosa, also dead. Most of his thinning hair had been disturbed by a large portion of his brain exploding into the air.

The walls of the big room I was in had been dismantled, revealing shelves loaded with bags of drugs. There were white bags, tan bags and green bags. All tightly sealed with the telltale plastic wrap.

Cocaine, heroin and marijuana.

So much for Dominique's "antiques."

No wonder she had planted the link between Wheels

and Villabosa. Her "client" was a drug dealer and she wanted her money. Which had probably been the case when she'd acted as Candyman's sidekick.

Suddenly, the big boat lurched and I knew someone had freed us from the dock and was taking us out to sea.

I stood, which was no easy feat. My head hurt. And the kick to the side had done more damage than I'd realized.

The first person I checked on was Drake. His gun was still in his hand.

"Money's money, right Drake?" I asked, and relieved him of his weapon. I checked the slide. One in the chamber. No sign of his girlfriend.

Man, I felt so much better with a gun in my hand.

I went back to where they'd tied me to the floor. There was another dead guy sprawled out in a semicircle of blood. One of Wheels's bodyguards.

The only people missing were Wheels and the Goth Girl.

And one thing I knew for certain.

Wheels hadn't made a run for it.

## 25

I left the main cabin of the boat and climbed the stairs to the deck. The boat was pointed out toward the middle of the sea, going at a slow cruise, with no one steering.

A piece of duct tape held the steering wheel in place.

The sound of a voice came through the night air and I stepped carefully out of the bridge, and saw a man draped over the side of the railing.

The Goth Girl was standing next to him.

She looked up at me, glanced at the gun in my hand.

And threw Wheels overboard.

We both heard the splash and then she walked toward me.

"You can say thank you at any time," she said.

I opened my mouth to say something and my breath caught in my throat.

The Goth Girl was lean, hard and utterly fearless. Her dark eyes shone in the night. She had just thrown a man overboard to his death and she looked as cool as the moonlight on her jet black hair.

For a moment, the eyes softened and she seemed amused.

Finally, my vocal cords managed to work just long enough to produce a single sound.

"Jenny," I said.

She nodded and replied.

"Hey, brother."

## 26

S he removed the duct tape from the steering wheel, tapped a navigation screen and leaned against the white leather captain's chair.

"I've been looking for you," I said.

"I know."

My phone was still in my pocket and it buzzed. It was Dominique. I decided not to answer. Not until I found out who she really was.

"For years," I added.

"I know," she replied. "Subtlety isn't your strong suit."

It was shocking to me. All these years I had searched for her, and worried about her, and now here she was.

"I can't believe I found you," I said.

"You didn't. I found you."

For the first time in a long time, maybe my whole life, I had no idea what the hell I was supposed to do.

"What–" I started to ask, and then stopped.

None of this was what I had imagined. I thought she was in trouble, and needed my help. Over the years, all sorts of crazy scenarios had run through my head. As it turned out, the reality was even more insane.

The helpless big sister I'd imagined had just killed three men right in front of me and saved my life.

"You don't want to know," she said, in response to the beginning of my question. "Besides, I wouldn't tell you, anyway."

Fair enough.

"Why?" I asked. "Why did you save my life?"

She leaned over the steering wheel, and rammed the throttle forward. Either we had gotten into deeper water where we could speed up, or she wanted this boat ride to go as fast as possible.

"It was a big contract," she said. "I knew you could take care of yourself, but the odds were against you."

This woman before me was my sister, but she also wasn't.

"Thank you," I said.

The hint of emotion seemed to intensify her, like a knife blade after one final sweep of the whetstone.

"Just business," Jenny said. "I did something for you, so you can assist me with a small matter."

It was interesting she used the word 'assist.' Apparently, even saying the word 'help' was not appealing to her. It was a window into what my sister had become, and what she had probably gone through.

"You name it," I said.

She folded her arms across her slender midsection.

"First, we need to dump all those bodies down there overboard."

"No problem."

She took a deep breath. It was still hard to believe this

woman was my sister. She was, there was no doubt. But she was so...hard.

I could see she was having a little trouble getting to the next part, so I helped her out.

"Anything. Just name it."

"They have my daughter," she finally said. "There are too many of them for one person. I needed someone who can spill a lot of blood. Someone I can trust."

Once again, I found myself at a loss for words.

My sister had a daughter.

"How old is she?" I asked.

"Four."

Behind us, the lights of the Bahamas slipped under the horizon. Out here, it was pitch black as we would soon hit the Gulf Stream. The most powerful ocean current on earth.

"What's her name?" I asked.

Jenny uncrossed her arms and gripped the boat's steering wheel. The muscles on her arms undulated and her knuckles turned white.

This time, it seemed like her vocal cords were having trouble functioning.

But finally, they produced a name.

"Angel."

# WADE CARVER THRILLER #3!

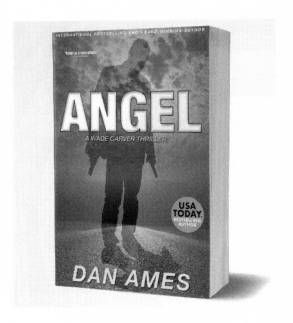

AuthorDanAmes.com

# ABOUT THE AUTHOR

Dan Ames is a USA TODAY Bestselling Author and winner of the Independent Book Award for Crime Fiction.

www.authordanames.com
dan@authordanames.com

**A USA TODAY BESTSELLING BOOK**

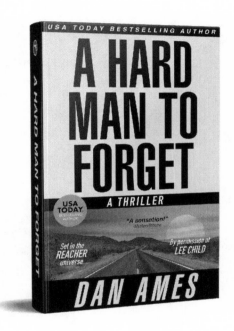

The JACK REACHER Cases

## ALSO BY DAN AMES

The JACK REACHER Cases #1 (A Hard Man To Forget)
The JACK REACHER Cases #2 (The Right Man For Revenge)
The JACK REACHER Cases #3 (A Man Made For Killing)

DEAD WOOD (John Rockne Mystery #1)
HARD ROCK (John Rockne Mystery #2)
COLD JADE (John Rockne Mystery #3)
LONG SHOT (John Rockne Mystery #4)
EASY PREY (John Rockne Mystery #5)
BODY BLOW (John Rockne Mystery #6)

THE KILLING LEAGUE (Wallace Mack Thriller #1)
THE MURDER STORE (Wallace Mack Thriller #2)
FINDERS KILLERS (Wallace Mack Thriller #3)

DEATH BY SARCASM (Mary Cooper Mystery #1)
MURDER WITH SARCASTIC INTENT (Mary Cooper Mystery #2)
GROSS SARCASTIC HOMICIDE (Mary Cooper Mystery #3)

KILLER GROOVE (Rockne & Cooper Mystery #1)

BEER MONEY (Burr Ashland Mystery #1)

THE CIRCUIT RIDER (Circuit Rider #1)

KILLER'S DRAW (Circuit Rider #2)

TO FIND A MOUNTAIN (A WWII Thriller)

STANDALONE THRILLERS:

THE RECRUITER

KILLING THE RAT

HEAD SHOT

THE BUTCHER

BOX SETS:

AMES TO KILL

GROSSE POINTE PULP

GROSSE POINTE PULP 2

TOTAL SARCASM

WALLACE MACK THRILLER COLLECTION

SHORT STORIES:

THE GARBAGE COLLECTOR

BULLET RIVER

SCHOOL GIRL

HANGING CURVE

SCALE OF JUSTICE

# FREE BOOKS AND MORE

Would you like a FREE copy
of my story BULLET RIVER?

Then sign up for the DAN AMES BOOK CLUB:

AuthorDanAmes.com

Made in United States
Orlando, FL
28 March 2024

45205454R00062